SHORT TIME

FRED MISURELLA

BORDIGHERA
WEST LAFAYETTE, IN

Library of Congress Cataloging-in-Publication Data

Misurella, Fred, 1940-
    Short Time / by Fred Misurella.
        p.   cm.
    ISBN 1-884419-07-0 (alk. paper)
    I. Title.
PS3563.I7353S55   1996
813'.54—dc21
                                                    96-46780
                                                    CIP

SHORT TIME was written with the help of a grant from the Commonwealth of Pennsylvania Commission on the Arts.

•

Thanks to Victoria Cays for her work on the cover and illustrations and to Ed Mendez for putting it all on disk.

Printed in the United States.

Published by
BORDIGHERA, INC.
Purdue University
1359 Stanley Coulter Hall
West Lafayette, IN 47907-1359

VIA FOLIOS 8
ISBN 1-884419-07-0

For Kim and Alex, with love.

(And for Jim Harms, Lori Blair, and Ralph Vitello,
good friends who love to read.)

"And in the end, of course,
a true war story is never about war."

—Tim O'Brien

TABLE OF CONTENTS

I

"Did you kill anyone over there?"

I stare at my daughter, speechless, frozen into a look, a pose, that I do not enjoy, although it protects me a little from her questions while I think. "I didn't go over there to run footraces or build muscles. But I didn't take potshots at the natives either."

She nods, props her sneakers on the rungs of a chair, puffs a cigarette, even though I remind her daily that with all her exercise the smoking doesn't make sense. Mayra is not hostile, or surprised. Rather she seems to acknowledge with her look the fact that I have—what?—taken part in, fully enjoyed, even revelled in, something that, as her father, I would never approve for her and that, besides, makes smoking the equivalent of a dieter digging into a second scoop of chocolate ice cream.

"I was used," I tell her. "They trained a killer, pushed a button, and then dumped me aside when the tallies had to be taken."

She stares. "Tallies?"

"Bodies—with no thought of the bloodshed or suffering involved. They wanted a clean war they could write about in high school history books, but they encouraged a dirty one instead. And they asked us to pretend that it had been clean."

Mayra smiles, shaking out her disheveled dark brown hair. I am lucky in my daughter. With all the confusion of these past twenty or twenty-five years, with all these raps about chauvinistic men, lesbian women, violent, abusive fathers, military atrocities, the divorce case her mother won against me, bad music, drugs, and God knows what the hell goes on in schools, she's a good kid—not starry-eyed, like I was, but good. More important, she loves me, and I think I even make her proud sometimes.

1

"Sometimes you talk as if it was a party," she says. "As if you were just invited. Yet you volunteered; you knew what you were getting into. . ."

She stops.

"No. No, I didn't. You are never prepared. It's too ugly. Too awful. The daily experience is just too much. You ask yourself, what kind of life is this I'm living? Am I living?"

She turns, staring out the window on a fine spring day: snow has completely vanished, woods next to the house are greening, geese honk on a pond just a quarter of a mile away. Mayra planted crocuses outside the window last year, and a dozen or more of them bloom now, their purple, yellow, and orange cups a welcome patch of color against the muddy soil. We also turned over a garden in the back, a twenty by thirty plot of lettuce, herbs, beans, tomatoes, zucchini, and asparagus that kept me vegetarian through most of last summer and fall. She loves these things, plans to study environmental science at college next year, and dreams of a house surrounded by acres of woods. She cannot understand that fields and trees are not necessarily good for me.

"It's the life we make of it, I guess," Mayra says. "If we control it."

"If we *can* control it, you mean. You don't know what I've seen. You don't know how much loss you can sustain."

She nods. "I can imagine, Daddy." She smiles, warmly, crushing her cigarette in an ashtray as she lets out a last full stream of smoke. "Living provides the opportunity, I guess."

Her mother, Valerie, and I stopped getting along definitively the night we married. If you ask me why, I'll say it's because we didn't really want to get married. If you ask Valerie, it will be because I demanded too much of her time and space. She is a social research scientist now, studying drugs, disease, and poverty to see how they affect people's lives. Once she cringed at scientists, believed in mind over matter and the body's natural power to heal itself. She wore jeans or long, loose-fitting dresses, embroidered cotton shirts with no bras or shaved armpits under them, hair down to her waist, and loved to tell fortunes or work through garden mud in bare feet and a straw hat that made her look like some of the peasants I saw in Vietnam. I was a catch for her, I suppose: We had known each other for about a year and split up. I joined the ROTC and, at graduation, volunteered to go to Vietnam. But upon my return there I was, for her, a vet without attitude who had come back to a college town and somehow for those days managed to keep himself quiet while the protests raged. For me Valerie was . . . I don't know. She was something I really could not understand.

We made love—the first time in years—on my parents' living room couch beneath a picture of cherry trees in blossom on the night my father, after an illness, collapsed from a stroke. He had entered the hospital for an examination that morning, and seemed alright, although the results from a couple of the tests would not be clear for a day or two. We had gone out to play cards at the Italian-American Club, and I had picked up Valerie after staying with him through the first couple of hands. Valerie and I went to a movie, drank beer at a local bar, and returned to my house. I had never brought a woman home before, let alone make love with her in the living room. But my mother was dead. My brother Sal lived with his girl on the other side of town. My sister Cora was married and lived with her family. And I knew my father would stay out late at the club. Besides, I must say, I needed the edge of danger for anything sexual to happen between me and women, especially someone I knew before, like Valerie.

Nothing had seemed right since I came back from Vietnam. I had gone on a drug and drinking binge for about a month—a period of absolute blankness in my memory—and when I came up, or out, because of Sal's, my father's, and Cora's urging, I passed weeks in a cloud of withdrawal that I hardly remember any better than the month on drugs. One day, finally, I saw where I was. As if I blinked, I looked around me, recognized I wasn't at home, realized my arms and legs were strapped down, saw the nurse in the corner dressed in neutral gray and white, and felt vaguely, comfortably, guilty, as if I had overslept, and with nothing critical missed. It took me just two weeks to leave the hospital, but it was months and months of an absolute deadness in my limbs, my thinking, my soul before I could minimally function. Writing letters helped—especially to old friends from college. And then it was a year or more—that night with Valerie beneath those painted trees—before I felt anything remotely like a normal, living need. My mother's ghost seemed to hover over us all through the hour on the couch, and the spookiness seemed confirmed when, as Valerie and I dressed around midnight, I received a phone call from the club saying my father had suffered an apparent stroke and an ambulance had taken him to the hospital.

He died just a month after that. Sal and his girl left to study in California, Cora bought a house in Connecticut with her husband, and Valerie moved into the family house with me. She is the adopted daughter of a Chinese-American, a real estate tycoon in California who had actually marched with Mao in the 1940s. She hated her father and his turncoat politics, envying him his American success since it gave her an almost impossible task of proving herself by comparison. She would gain revenge, she would make a failure of her life to make up for the aloofness and disdain he had meted out to her because she was adopted, liberal, and female. Where I fit in, I really can't say. Maybe the fact that I had fought communists, killed and maimed Vietnamese, travelled to the Orient to see and conquer. . . I don't know, maybe that said something to her—or to her father. For me she was in some sense a justification, and a vindication, of everything I had been—especially in Nam.

We stayed in my parents' house until the following spring when Cora, Sal, and I held a telephone meeting and decided to sell everything. We split the profits plus a few mementos, and then Valerie and I left for a month or two of wandering in

Europe until that fall when "we," as she used to say, got pregnant. About to begin graduate school, she did not want the baby, and we fought about it all through the flight to the United States and the two weeks following while we looked for a hospital and doctor. We settled into our own apartment, and then immediately, brought on by the move, the fights, or the trip from Europe, suffered a miscarriage that Christmas. The experience was horrible, and there was no one to blame—not the President, not the media, not the "power structure," not the VC pigs or a stupid general. It was biology; it was God.

It changed Valerie, replaced her faith in nature with a profound distrust, and while we married, got pregnant again within six months, and then delivered Mayra in a thrilling, trouble-free Lamas style birthing just nine months later, she was never quite the same. She seemed to oppose everything, including life, after that, assault nature with strategies of chemicals, prophylactics, and sprays, until, with Mayra at last in school, she decided to return to graduate school for a degree in social work. I began graduate studies part time and, with the infant Mayra in tow, we moved to a comfortable little university town where my wife studied full time and I, between my own classes, minded baby and diapers and tried to earn a living for all of us by frying hash and eggs and bacon at the local diner. "We" got pregnant again, but Valerie absolutely refused to have it. We fought for weeks and separated. She had a change of heart, but one day in the fourth or fifth month, while I was at work, she packed her clothes and Mayra's and left town.

At the family planning clinic, they knew nothing about her, although the woman on the phone informed me that even if they did it would be highly unusual for them to tell me anything, given who I was. I drove west to Valerie's parents, following her to Los Angeles I thought, but her mother had neither seen nor heard from her in days. I went to San Francisco to see her sister, and she told me the same thing. After two weeks, I returned to my job at the diner. The police turned up nothing for several months, and then one day I received a letter from Valerie. It was postmarked from Florida, and in it she told me she had given birth to a boy and turned it over to religious authorities for adoption. She and Mayra had moved on to another state where she was working and trying to find her way back into graduate school. She and Mayra were fine, but any money I could send would certainly help. She would spend it only on what Mayra needed, none of it on herself. As always, I trusted her. I wrote out a check for twenty-five dollars and dropped it in the mail.

"A huge drop of ink mixing with a bowl of water"

II

"Anatomy is destiny," Freud said in one of his essays, tying it up, as I remember, with some other idea like the absence of a penis, the desire to piss out fire or kill your father. Other than through my reading in college, I haven't had much contact with that sort of stuff, always having loved my mother and father sincerely, never wanting to harm either, not even in a moment of anger, and never expecting any more from the plumbing between my legs than the opportunity through love or promises to extend my anatomical presence into another being, to connect with a woman if she and the moment were right, and, later, to create a child if larger, more mysterious forces than my promises agreed.

Still, I admit, I volunteered for Nam, volunteered for combat, and took pride that of the hundreds of thousands over there, I was one of the rare, and I must say privileged, thousands to have gone out on the hunt for fire. There were three kinds of grunts in Nam: the reluctant ones who regretted every moment in the field; the eager who loved to fight to make something of themselves, or to make up for something missing in themselves; and the rest, a narrow majority, I believe, who simply went out to fight because they loved their country, this was war, and they had the quiet faith to know that, win or lose, they could do it, not greatly, but well. And that was how I saw myself: average, caught up in a world turning ugly against my wishes. My father had not fought in World War II; he had worked in a defense-related industry instead. None of his brothers had fought, and his radical father had joined some sort of pacifist, socialist alliance that somehow made him unfit for World War I in Italy. And my own brother, Sal, god knows, had done everything short of crossing the border to avoid the war. Whatever he did, it worked. Once he registered at seventeen, he never even heard from our draft board again, not in 1965, not in '68 (a year after I left for Vietnam); not in 1970 or later, when the draft lottery went into effect.

So, unlike a lot of guys I met in country, I had no pressure to join up from a family tradition. But the feeling was in there, inside me, whether from books, movies, or tv, I'll never know. I just felt that I had to go, as if I owed something. Call it my anatomy if you will, but I thought I'd never be happy with myself if I stayed home. I could have taken a job helping the poor (plenty of my friends had done that), or gone to graduate school, earned another degree, and taught. Instead, I saw an image of me in combat boots and fatigues with a rifle in my hand, and despite all the doubts of my mother and Cora, the laughter and scorn of my brother Sal, I felt I needed to make that image real. And it was more than feeling and need. It was knowledge and inevitability. I had no idea what came after that bright, self-contained image I saw, but it was a self that would continue to torment me whether I wanted it to or not (I didn't want it to). More important, I knew it as the most positive image of myself I was ever likely to see.

To my surprise, and for one of the few times in my life, my imagination was right: I turned out to be a damn fine soldier, one of the kind a company depends on, the kind his fellow soldiers respect and his commanders like. I volunteered for search and destroy, rescue missions, and reconnaissance. I marched quietly, tending to business, never hot-dogged or otherwise blew the company's cool. I received commendation for valor twice, led my units with a minimal loss of men and a minimal loss of discipline among the men, and so when Tet hit in early 1968, mine was one of the few company units not to lose a man, not to give up a foot of turf when the fire erupted in our zone.

I still wonder about it. Freud says men are natural killers and rapists, I think, holding back their aggression to build cities and nations, to write songs and shape their futures. But what about us, and there are many, who give in to their anatomy for a period in their lives, or for a moment, and somehow see a different vision? That morning of Tet, a quiet, warm dawn, as I recall, with clouds above the mountains turning the sun into a ghostly lavender shade, erupted into a battle that didn't stop (for me) for several years. Camped in a field near a village not many miles from the mountains, I walked through some thick brush toward a river I could wash in and, as I had the day before, stopped on this little pile of red earth to look at the sky. It was dangerous, but we had cleaned out the zone a week before. Besides, I love the morning, always feel secure in it, and felt an inner need to stand on that hill, turn a circle with a rifle and canteen in my hands, and take it all in: the conical mountains, the wide gaps between them, the village lights on the fields to their left and right, the lush growth of trees and brush behind me, and a single, narrow gap, this one through the trees, of a path on the way to fresh water.

"What a morning!" I whispered, seeing the mountains, the trees behind me, and the lavender light just spreading across the clouds and sky like a huge drop of ink mixing with a bowl of water. I heard a rustle to my right, dropped to one knee, and raised the rifle to see a little village dog, white, short-haired, with a black patch over one of its eyes, emerge from the underbrush and after a short stop head straight up the hill toward me. I studied the brush to its left and right, and behind me, seeing no other movement. It paused about ten feet away, swinging its head to the right and wagging its tail as if to ask my permission to come closer. It was thin, obviously underfed, with ribs prominent through its skin. I studied the brush again, feeling terribly vulnerable in that place, and, not wanting to make too loud a sound, waved the barrel of the rifle to send the dog away. It whimpered, lay down, and rolled over as if by my command. On its feet again, it stepped closer, wagging its tail and staring into my eyes as if begging me to take it in. I waved the rifle again, and this time it lay on its back and wagged its tail. I walked down the hill toward the gap in the trees and, rifle ready, headed for the water.

The dog ran ahead, obviously knowing the trail, and, with stops to sniffle and pee, led me into the brush until we were surrounded by trees and shade. I was spooked, I admit, feeling the dog was a trap, leading me somewhere I didn't want to go, even though it headed in the same direction I had intended. A warm breeze blew through the dark brush, and I kept reminding myself that we controlled the area. We had cleaned it out just two days ago and were, definitively, in charge. No one unfriendly should have been within a mile without me knowing it. Of course you know, as I did then, that by the order of some fun-loving, or hateful, god, thinking like that often leads humans into trouble.

The path led directly to the river. The dog followed it, stopping as we got to the banks to sniff at a stump and the rump end of a pile of wood. I glanced around, rifle still poised, and emerged from the overhang of trees. Like so many rivers I had seen in Nam, this one flowed muddy and deep, and there were times when the men really didn't want the water. But a few feet from the banks, the water flowed more clearly, and so, if you felt lucky, you could risk finding something better.

Just out from the brush, I looked at the trees across the way. Even with the sun behind me, shining into those trees, I saw nothing, and with the dog sniffing at the trees and stump without suspicion, I decided to take the chance, especially since I knew the bank wasn't steep at all. Fully clothed, with the rifle and canteen above my waist, I slipped my boots into the water, sank into the mud until I found a couple of stones to stand on, and then, resisting the current, gradually strode down and along the embankment until, about twenty-five feet out, the river rose to my armpits. Water ran clear out there. As I lowered my canteen into it, I looked around: The sun shone above the trees behind me now; near the banks of a little peninsula down river a silver-colored bird, a crane or heron probably, stood in the water, one foot lifted, and seemed to listen for movement. It dunked its head, came up with nothing, and, after a sidelong glance at something on the peninsula, spread its wings and lifted off. Spooked myself, I waded back toward land, scanning the landscape on either side of the river, and feeling only slightly more comfortable when I saw the dog still at its original spot.

Dripping, I capped the canteen. I had lost nearly a quarter of its contents on the way back but didn't care. I took cover in the trees, stopped at the edge of the clearing to glance around, and still saw nothing. Another water bird, light turning its silver colors golden, grazed near the opposite shore now, and I started back for the camp after another few minutes of staring. The dog ran ahead of me and led the way. We came to a fork in the road that I had often wondered about. One path led back to the camp, and the other I didn't know. I had followed it for a few yards once on reconnaissance and knew that it was overgrown, winding through a marshy, open field with hills on either side. I didn't know where it led, although I suspected, from our maps, that it turned back to the original path. The dog took the fork, stopped when I looked after it and hesitated, and then simply put its nose to the ground and plunged on. I took the original way but, after a few steps, felt I shouldn't. What kind of officer wouldn't completely know the territory he and his men guarded? What kind of security did we have if I didn't know this path between two dots in our recon packs?

Without thinking further, I turned, making sure my rifle was dry, and plunged after the dog onto that second path. The woods and brush were thicker here. The path curved off to the left, skirted a paddy, and, muddy there, pointed toward some other woods where it entered the trees and brush again. I saw no new footprints, no sign of life except the dog and its paws. But as we moved closer to the trees, another path crossed this one from the direction of the river, and at that junction I saw fresh human prints, not from Marine-issue boots but retread tire sandals that must have turned outward with each step, scooping up a delta of mud and clay with the arch side of the sandals. I felt myself crouch automatically, keeping the rifle ready at my chest, and followed slowly, quietly as I could, behind those prints. I heard nothing, not a voice, not the sound of any animal. The dog dropped back a few steps, its nose closer to the earth as it sniffed each little mound the sandals left, and then as we walked beneath the trees, glanced back at me and darted forward. I took two or three steps to follow, arrived at a curve, crouched lower as I took two more steps, and saw the back of a man in front of me, walking in the same direction.

His shoulders slumped forward, his head inclined toward the mud he trudged through. He wore black pajamas, a straw papa-san hat, and seemed to carry something, I wasn't sure what, in his arms. The dog caught up with him, barked, circled his feet, and leaped on his hip with great delight. I fell to my knee, seeing the man stop and turn toward me. He moved quickly. I saw the dark barrel of his rifle—almost lost in the darker cloth of his pajama top—and with my own M-16 already at my shoulder, I centered the hairs on his chest and squeezed the trigger.

"Peace . . . without the ground blowing up beneath my feet"

III

"Blown away," the Top said to me. "Completely. But you had to do it. How could you tell?"

I had run back to the hooch, still seeing the surprised look, the hat flying like a conical saucer, the pajama top exploding with the blood, the frail body lifted out of its sandals and almost out of its trousers, and the dog, wailing, plunging into the underbrush, running evasive patterns through the trees. After a few seconds, I retreated to the clearing and, on my stomach, checked out the paddy and the hills beyond. I saw nothing. Returning to the body again, I took another look along the path and through the trees. Again, nothing. I looked down, saw the legs twisted as if to run in the opposite direction of the trunk, and then, checking for identification, I noticed two things: the "barrel" didn't extend from a rifle but was a farm tool, a hoe of some kind, and the "chest" I had blown out of its shirt held the remnants of two breasts with a woman's nipples on them.

Later, I sat on my cot with my head in my hands and tried to understand what happened. I knew I had acted properly, although perhaps a little hastily, and that even a peasant woman might have been dangerous, armed or not, because she might give information to others. But I had been very careful up to that point, keeping the men of my platoon under tight control, never allowing them to take the slightest chance on injuring peaceful people, men as well as women. I had succeeded in keeping our record clean of any atrocities, and in fact, despite the snide remarks of a couple of my regulars, I had impressed on the men the need to represent our country well: "If we're fighting to make them friends," I told the men, "we damn well have to make them *want* to be our friends, especially while we're fighting on their land."

And I had done well, proud of my platoon's record in battle

15

and my own record as their leader. You've heard the stories. The burned villages are nothing, almost excusable, because in fact the men couldn't know what was hidden inside the huts, or beneath them. The personal, individual injuries were worse: Soldiers taking target practice at peasants working in a field; grunts forcing grenades down a valuable working cow's throat; men viciously raping whole families of women and then killing them. Those are the stories we've brought back, admit to. For every one of those there must be hundreds unreported and, maybe, worse.

But I had steered clear of that as best I could, made my men avoid it too. Yet now, as if it were a mine, I had stepped onto it by accident. We controlled the area, but by no means knew all the people in it. So it was hard to know who this young woman was, whether in fact she lived around here, and if, as my gut said she did, she had a family. I wanted to make retribution, pitiful as that might seem, and so, after a half hour or so in the hooch, I left the Top in charge and walked back to the overhang to look around.

At the path I saw no new footprints, just the narrow bump, bump, bump of the little crescent moons her sandals had left. Blood had drained from her. Flies cruised from her mouth to her wound, to her nose and then her wide-open eyes. Without thinking, I looked at her hands, but I had never seen a ring on any of these people, married or not. She carried no papers, and when I looked inside her clothes and hat, even at the hoe, I found no writing, nothing to identify her in any way.

I continued along the path, hoping to find a field, a hut, or possibly a little village. Unlike the first trip, I felt no fear, not even a sense of caution. I might have walked into a minefield for all I knew. But, even at a step away from losing everything, I could only see that woman's face when I shot her. Sometimes I thought of Cora, sometimes of my mother, and once or twice, with irony, I thought of my brother Sal, of the smart remarks he might make.

The path went through a paddy, skirted another overhang of trees, passed a muddy, foul-smelling field, and led up to a group of five or six huts that we had not known about. Three men and a woman in black pajamas worked in a paddy just beyond the huts, and a couple of older women watched some kids playing behind them. I walked slowly, rifle up, but reluctantly, watching the huts, and hoping to make some kind of peace with these people without the ground blowing up beneath my feet. The two older women stopped talking and stared at me. Then the kids stopped, and one of them called out to the men and woman in the paddy. Slowly, I took a white handkerchief out of my pocket and waved it. They did not respond. As I came closer, the two men in the paddy walked toward the huts, arriving near the old women and children just as I did.

"Hello," I said.

"*Howa*," one of them said, a mix, as I imagined it, of "hello," "hi," and "how." One of the men, obviously nervous, waved his hand. I have read a good deal about how beautiful the Vietnamese are, but very little about the hardness you can see on their faces. It's a look that says they expect nothing and will give nothing, having nothing to give or expect. They work hard. We used to see them bending over the paddies for hours, never standing straight as they walked from rice plant to rice plant all day long, dawn to sunset. They speak little, even among themselves, at least when strangers are around. So, the man's nervous show of friendliness made me wary. "GI welcome," he said. "America number one."

Holding up a thumb, he laughed, and the whole group of them did the same.

"Are you all here?" I said, trying to sound official. "Anyone missing?"

The man frowned, eyeing the rifle and my lieutenant's stripes. The four of them fell into a conversation I could not follow. They pointed in several directions at once, waved their hands, said "Number one" a couple of times, and, finally, the smiler shook his head.

"Woman gone . . . hoe?" I said, raking at the ground with my rifle butt.

They shook their heads, unsmiling. "No hoe," one of the older women said and shook her head again. A crane circled overhead, its neck in an s-curve, its legs dragging behind as if on a separate current. For a moment we all studied it, and then the smiling man touched my sleeve, raising his hands when I quickly stepped away. "American GI," he said, raising his thumb again. "Number one."

I took his sleeve, trying to look sincere, friendly, and in charge at the same time. "Come," I said. "You come with me." He looked at the others, shrugged his shoulders, and raised his hands. But he didn't budge. He and the others talked and the women shook their heads. I tugged his sleeve again, not letting go this time, and made sure to pull him with me as I walked. The other man and the two women followed, first sending the children into the fields where the lone woman and man stood and watched, motionless.

We followed the path through the overhang, past the two paddies and the smelly field, and came to the overgrown path where the woman lay. The four of them remained silent, as I did, their eyes wide but not fearful, their behavior remarkably composed, I thought, considering that I carried the rifle. Occasionally they whispered something to each other. It was nothing that I could understand, but at the same time they showed little sense of fear, even as we turned a bend and saw that body sprawled out about sixty yards ahead. At that point the four of them stopped, looked quickly at each other then at me. Their expressions changed, but I could not really say how. Maybe it was just the responsible, final presence of the dead. Probably it was more personal. The serious man whispered something to the others and all four forged ahead. The women went first, the men lagging behind, but all just ahead of me as I followed and made 360 degree turns with my eyes and the M-16.

They ran for a bit, talking quickly, then stopped about ten yards away from the body and, silent again, circled it.

"Do you know her?" I said. "From your village?"

They stared at her a long time, not saying anything to each other or me. The smiling one covered his eyes and looked away. One of the old women spit into the dirt near the corpse's foot and rubbed her hands together. The other woman, with an incredibly strong, if wrinkled face, shook her head. I looked hard into the thick brush, saw no sign of that spotted dog, and, loudly, asked them again if they knew her. I mentioned the dog, but that said nothing to them. The serious one began to speak, but when he saw I didn't understand anything raised both his hands and repeated "G.I. number one" several times. All four repeated that, the women less convincingly, I thought, and when one of them looked down the path behind me, I spun around and dropped to one knee. With my rifle at my shoulder, I saw one of the little kids. But before I could do or say anything, the two old women fell to their knees in front of me and tried to grab the M-16 barrel. The two men patted my shoulders and made me understand that nothing was wrong, at least nothing worth shooting a rifle over. They smiled, trying to point the barrel into the air. Furious, I stood, shoved the rifle in the smiling one's face and, telling them to stop, made them all raise their hands above their heads. I felt scared, super, super spooked. I did not like all those people surrounding me. Backing away, I started toward the river and the camp. Passing the corpse, I reached into my pocket and, half wanting to rub their noses in it, pulled out some coins and threw them on the ground. They said and did nothing. I continued to back away, staring into the brush and hills all around, and finally, at the bend where I had seen her, turned and ran. The last thing I saw was the child in the smiling man's arms and the strong, wrinkled woman on her knees before the corpse. She wasn't gathering money. With her hand to her face, she bobbed her head forward and backward, almost touching the ground. I thought I heard her scream.

"Leaving something behind, I would be different"

IV

That afternoon the VC hit us with everything: mortar, rocket shells, rifle fire. As we set up defenses to repel them and reconned to try to track them down, the earth shook beneath our feet, trees exploded, the night sky turned treacherous as mud, rock, and roots plunged over and around us, as well as through some unlucky others. The attack made us forget everything except the most primitive responses—dip, dodge, dive, the muscular descent into darkness and security. I forgot that woman and her death, I forgot that family of peasants and my coins. For a certain time I also forgot who I was—name, serial number, everything. But I am a little ashamed to say that my sense of rank and responsibility never left. I kept my men together, gave clear directives, made them act orderly even under stress, forcing them to remember that we were Marines, American Marines, and as such had an important job we could not foul up, especially now.

They responded beautifully, as I knew they would, calling in mortars and air strikes of our own, securing the area within three hundred yards of the camp, and knocking down a verifiable eighty-five or one hundred of the enemy within forty-eight hours. I have read that the VC Tet offensive of 1968, militarily, at least, was a failure, and I can only say that according to what I saw and experienced that assessment is accurate. Our company gave no quarter, lost no territory, almost no equipment, and not one man. In addition to the ones we killed, we captured more than fifty of the VC themselves. Toward the end of the first three days, I began to look at enemy faces again, hoping to catch a glimpse, for self-justification, of one of the village peasants I had left on the trail. But, in all honesty, I think I had already forgot what they looked like. I could never pick anyone out. What's more, I never got back to the village to see how they were because, although I reported the presence of that village and the killing of the woman in the path, our platoon never had the time to march into the area and control it, at least not under my command. About three weeks after the attacks began, when things were mostly under control again and we were pounding butt to keep things orderly on the new LZ, we received orders to recon that village. My platoon was leaving that very afternoon, after a morning of loading supplies, but then the Top walked up to bring me another, uglier, piece of news.

"Lieutenant, Sir."

"Top. You're not bringing me new casualty figures, I hope. I'm tired of them."

"No, sir."

"Or new offensive plans. God knows we're hurt enough as it is. I don't even want to go out into the field."

"No, sir. No new plans."

"Discipline?"

"It's nothing like that, sir. Nothing military at all."

"Good, cause I'd just as soon hear about the Phils or the Pirates as goddamn VC today."

The sergeant lowered his head and shook it. "Nothing like that either, sir, I'm afraid."

I glanced over at a dusty six-by rumbling toward us with supplies—food, equipment, the thousands of rounds of ammunition we spent every day—even without the VC attacking us in waves. "Well, what is it then?"

He said nothing. I watched the six-by driver pull to a halt, backing up to the doors of the Cobra. Some men put down their rifles, others turned about, staring alertly into the jungle for any unusual movement.

"Well, Top, what is—"

I glanced at him and saw his arm extended, a folded piece of yellow notepaper in his hand, "Red Cross" stamped on top. He continued to look down at his feet as I took the paper. I unfolded it, read the message, and waved to the six-by driver, pointing to a load of containers I wanted brought back. When he gave me the okay sign, I read the message again: "*Mother dead. Prepare to leave immediately.*"

"I'm sorry, sir."

I said nothing, wondering if it wasn't some bad company joke. I was on what we called "short time"; my combat duty was coming to an end, and I was ready to leave the war in another fifteen days. I checked the Top for a smile, but saw only his long, serious expression. Nodding, I thanked him for the news and asked when the message had come in. "Within the hour, sir. I brought it right over from the CQ. Captain says he'll get you out on the first helicopter he can. Jones will take over here, sir. You're to come right back with me."

"The war is over," I said.

He looked at me strangely.

"Can you wait a minute, Top?"

"Sure, Lieutenant. Whatever you like."

Thanking him, I walked toward the six-by, picked up some gear I had stashed near the Cobra, and after a quick, unsatisfying farewell to the men in my platoon, rode back to CQ with the Top Sergeant. There, the Captain informed me that a Cobra would leave for Saigon in an hour and emergency orders would be waiting for me there.

I went to the hooch, packed my gear, said good-bye to some friends, and within an hour was in a Cobra, hearing the ping of sniper fire against the fuselage and blades as they lifted us over the mountains and carried us south along the river. I said nothing to the crew. But they must have known something; they maintained a respectful silence as I looked out the window and, from time to time, glanced at the last letter from my mother. "At last," she had written, "it's decided. I'm going into the hospital next weekend and I'll have the operation on the following Monday. I want to get this over with so I can be well when you come home. Just two more months! If I get the operation now, the doctor says I'll be well enough. . . ."

I had received the letter just a few weeks before, on the morning before Tet. I had worried a little; but from the tone of my mother's letter nothing dramatic seemed imminent. I was in a period of my life where I tried to minimize worry where my loved-ones were concerned. My mother had not wanted me to join up; my father had. I had been sheltered, but now that I was twenty-four, had seen battle and, indeed, killed, I felt that if I let myself become frightened over my mother's health, I would never leave her in any permanent sense. I had the habit of suppressing feelings in relation to her, had joined the Marines as part of a personal campaign to cut the apron strings, "become a man," as we liked to say, and so, as I read her last letter on the way into Bien Hoa, I suppose I kept myself from feeling its effect. Instead, I concentrated on that woman, and the family, becoming resolved in some way that I had done the right thing. As I stood in the sun at the airport while waiting for my plane, I acted quietly sorry but, looking back on it now, pretty clear-headed. It just didn't seem real—neither my mother, nor that woman. The dead were torn apart, burned, suddenly shot as they popped a lude—or they were simply blown away during an act of carelessness. There was nothing you could do but try. It was a zone of happenstance. I had survived, others hadn't. But there would come a war, hot or cold, that would get me too. So I was detached, occasionally even buoyant at my good fortune that afternoon as the plane left the cement and metal of Saigon and leveled off over the Indian Ocean, carrying me toward America where, in less than forty-eight hours from the time the Top Sergeant held out the note, I stepped off the bus in my hometown.

Tired and relieved, I walked the two blocks from the bus station, stood a few minutes before the dark house, and, finally, rang the bell. I had to ring it a couple of times, knock once, and call out beneath a window in back before the lights went on. My father, in his undershorts, answered the door.

"Hi, Dad. How are you?"

"Oh, Nickie. . ." He waved and let me into the living room
before saying anything else. My father always struck me as
absurd in his underwear; now, after three years of khaki and
more than one of blood he seemed less so. He had a lanky body
with thin arms and legs, and a bulky middle dominated by a firm
paunch whose size amazed people, including himself. He
attributed the firmness to indigestion—gas, which, he claimed,
forced him to emit enormously loud farts that, with a chuckle
to this day, I remember as rifle shots or grenade explosions.
He had a standard story, told over and over through my youth,
that he was born farting instead of crying, and that his mother
said it had saved his life when he had colic. He wore boxer
shorts and strapped t-shirts as a rule, and his shorts flapped
like a clown's pantaloons when he walked, so that any bravado
he had always lost force by the memory of him stripped to his
underwear.

"Are you alone?" I asked. "Cora isn't here?"

"Naw, she went home to the kids. Sal is here—in your
room."

Sal, my younger brother, was eighteen years old, already
working and living on his own—and attending college. He would
be the one to spend time with my father, I thought.

"Dad, tell me . . . what happened?"

He waved again and turned to sit on a chair. I glanced
around the living room, immediately feeling uncomfortable.
The room was decorated completely to my mother's taste. There
was an old flowered sofa, a French provincial coffee table, a
leather-topped lamp stand that sat in the middle of a picture
window, and that large, idyllic print of blossoming cherry trees
with a gaudy, gilded frame. The print showed a small brook
behind the trees with grass on each bank, and pink on pink of
blossoms covering the grass, sky, and brook, turning everything
else into background. It was slightly religious at the same time
it was vacuous, and I'd often recalled it with irony when we

marched into darkly foliated jungles back in Nam. Vegetation was a trap back there. Here, within a frame, it gave our living room a sense of peace and space.

Dropping the duffle bag to the floor, I bent over my father, and embraced him, even though he tried to push me away.

"Don't," he said, letting his arms settle across his stomach. "Those goddamn doctors did us dirty."

He sat next to his desk, a tall secretary he had inherited from his father, and let his face fall into his hands. My stomach turned. He needed strength, I know, but as if I were speaking to a new recruit, I told him to buck up and be brave. The enormity of the situation had not fully touched me yet, I think, and when I tried to calm him in firm, soldierly tones, it only made him moan. Then the look on his face grabbed me at the heart.

"I—I'm sorry," I managed to blurt out while I looked at him. "I—I'm—"

He waved his hand, as if to push it all away. "We're all sorry. That was the best goddamn woman—"

There was real loss in his grief, and as his sobs smothered his words, I waited a few seconds, looking around the living room and wished I could push everything away. "Christ," I said at last. "I haven't seen a bed in two days. Can we talk about all this in the morning? I need a break."

He turned on the stairway light and allowed me to walk with him to his bedroom. When I went upstairs to my own room, the darkness seemed to close in on me. I sensed that the excitement I had been having for the past three years—or at least my feeling of excitement—had been youthful imagination. I had thought I was leaving something behind, that I might get hurt but at least I would be different. Yet as I turned on the small lamp in my room and saw my brother Sal in the twin bed next to my desk, I had the feeling that things were really staying the same. A car rolled down the street; in the distance I heard something that sounded like gunfire. I took off my clothes, whispered hello as Sal, turning and briefly looking my way, threw up a sleepy wave. I noted the long hair, the beads around his neck, and the unshaved woolliness on his chin. I turned off the light, smiling. Without thinking about it, I pulled the covers from the bed and, wrapping myself up in them, lay on the hard wood floor.

V

Despite my memories, I understand little of that period. My daughter, Mayra, seventeen, beautiful in spite of chopped and lacquered hair, insists that I have gone nowhere, that I "simply do not see," as she says it, and that for her no war is worth death, no death worth a life, no life worth the heartbreak that went into maiming it. "Child of the nineties," she calls herself, meaning that she is used to separation, the independence that comes from lack of family, the superficial sense that she and her peers are just one big—not necessarily happy, but very separate—world.

"Touchy-feely," she calls me—the sexual meaning secondary in her words. "I mean *feeling*. You and your people are always trying to emote."

She grins, her dark eyes (from her mother) sparkling, her nose in the air (also from her mother), her shining hair spiked and messy as she laces a pair of pumped-up workout shoes.

"'My people?' Who do you mean by that?"

She nods. "You know. Sixties, seventies. 'All We Need is Love', 'Let's Do it in the Road.' It's all so innocent—and phoney."

She laughs, stretching her legs as she rises, her haunches tight while she leans against my father's old desk chair. I can't stand the thought of her with men, especially boys her own age, the ones with clowny pants and shoes and designs razored into their hair. I worry about AIDS, pregnancy, rubbers that somehow fall apart or disappear.

"Don't break that," I say, pointing to the chair. "Loosen up on something stronger."

She switches to the wall and, after a minute stretching out each calf, walks to the front door. She is going to jog to a club I bought her a membership in and workout with an aerobics class. Her boyfriend will meet her there, pump himself up with the hardware my membership pays for, and, I am sure, in the wee, small hours of tomorrow morning, get naked with her before he drives her home. "I'll be careful," she says, before I can voice my caution. "I will stay away from cars, keep to the better lit districts, and not workout beyond my strength. I will keep warm, dry, and clean, and I assure you that Darth will use a condom. But you have to remember that some of that depends on mood."

She opens the door and stares into the evening. The sun has turned colors in the clouds above the trees. "Like lollipops," she says, stretching her arms out toward the horizon. "I want to take it all in."

"Tomorrow," I say. "Tomorrow night I want you to stay home with me."

She nods. "Is Darth invited?"

I nod. "If he wants to see the film."

"Film? Oh, God, the film I've been hearing about for years? I'm not sure what you want me to see."

"How we were."

"I've seen that before. Often." She frowns.

"No, you haven't. Not with my family. I want you to know. Then maybe next day I'll take you to the grave."

"Grave?"

"You know, your grandparents. You've never been there. I want you to see it."

She makes a face, runs her fingers through her hair, and puts on a pair of cotton gloves. Then, without so much as a nod, she steps into the twilight and closes the door. Who knows what men are down those lanes, among those trees, lying in wait for her with rage and death in their arms? I run out to the sidewalk, step into the driveway, and, my heart pounding in desperation, put up my hand and wave.

VI

Our family was not given to open displays of affection. We did few things together, and since my parents were not church-going Italian Catholics, we didn't even worship together. Bursts of anger and exasperation were more habitual than affection, and the only time I remember real, extended, joyful contact between my mother and father was at their twenty-fifth wedding anniversary, significantly an event that was captured on film and more significant perhaps because it was the one time I ever saw my father drunk. He was so drunk, in fact, that he had to leave the party early to go to bed, where he vomited and nearly choked himself to death. The only direct memory I have of the time is my father, pale and groggy, hands trembling as he tried to drink coffee next morning, his face whiter than the sugar on the doughnut he habitually dunked into his cup, and my mother, hardly sympathetic, warning me never to let myself drink that much.

The movie of that evening is different, and that is why I have wanted to show it to Mayra for so long. It is black and white, about fifteen minutes long, on cassette now with no sound or editing. The party was held in the basement of the huge two-family house that Sal, Cora, and I sold many years ago, only to see it knocked down to make way for condominiums.

My parents had bought it in 1949, and my father had remodeled part of the basement into a recreation and party room. It contained a ping pong table, a couple of couches, and two rows of benches along the walls. There were pictures of movie and sport stars on one wall, and a coconut painted to look like an Indian beside them. The anniversary film opens with a shot of the coconut, moves along the wall to a picture of Joe DiMaggio and, beside him, one of Lana Turner, then pans the room to photograph the family and guests. I'm chubby and cute in my shoot'em up cowboy hat and holster; Sal is smiling and sweet in his little Peter Rabbit pajamas; and Cora is sparkling and beautiful in her curly Jane Russell hair. Almost everyone, close and distant from the family was in attendance, and the camera registers all of them as it pans matter-of-factly, stopping at the far end again, where the table is now laid out as the party's center piece. There, beneath the picture of Joe Di and Lana, my mother and father stand in front of the anniversary cake. "Nick and Sophie, Twenty-five years," the camera tells us, "Happy Anniversary."

My father holds up the cake while the camera zooms in and back; then he sets it on the table and, taking a sly look at my mother, sticks his finger into the frosting and licks it off. She slaps his hand, and to the shouting and laughter that must have followed, he grabs her shoulders and plants a creamy, frosting-layered kiss on her mouth. She shoves him away, wiping her mouth. He kisses her again to, what I gather from the looks on their faces, is general merriment.

My mother takes a knife, slices it expertly into the cake, cuts the first piece, and lifts it out to feed my father. His eyes shine confidently, glint naughtily in a way that shows he knows his manner pleases. He takes a section of the piece and feeds it to my mother—who baked the cake, I believe, although it was Aunt Carol who probably did the decoration. When my mother bites the cake, she makes exaggerated, smacking motions with her lips. The camera shows her as plain, with premature gray hair combed straight back from her forehead, and, because of her shame over two missing front teeth, a close-lipped smile. Whatever the reason, the film shows clearly that although I remember her strength and sobriety throughout our life, and eventually tried to copy it, my father was the free-spirited, attractive one having a good time. That's all: a few cheap feels from him, he laughs; a few embarrassed, tight-lipped smiles from her, and I still feel my heart stop (and see the note the Top put in my hand) when the movie ends abruptly in a shower of light: My mother cuts the cake. We see it passed out to the rest of the party as snow begins to dot the screen, spreads, sticks, and eventually, before one bite is taken, turns it white.

VII

I had mixed feelings as Sal drove my father and me down to the funeral home the day after my arrival. The undertaker was a man I had known since elementary school. He had always been a skinny, ratty looking boy, and because of his family's business we used to call him "Digger," or "Digger Di," although his family name was simply Maggio, after the month of May. Young, neat-looking that morning, he wore glasses, carried himself bent slightly from the waist, his hands folded before him as if he anticipated something with pleasure. He showed us the viewing room, and to my relief said my mother "was not ready," but we could see her that afternoon. He also told us that my mother's favorite priest, Father Peter Rossi, would be there and that he would conduct a service for her. I said nothing then, but secretly I felt numb. I had for so long seen life as cheap, not really to be desired, and I felt that funerals, especially those with religious services were hypocritical. Sure it was tradition, family, Catholic, and Italian, but I had seen a different world and wanted it recognized by the others. It wasn't until Cora arrived that afternoon to talk over arrangements with Sal and me that I said anything.

"Why do we need a priest? Why can't we just wrap her in a blanket and bury her in the backyard, or cremate her?"

"In the backyard? Are you crazy?" Cora said.

"Dad wants it this way," Sal said. "They were raised in the Church, married in it, so. . ."

"Oh, God, why do we need *anything*? If we need a sermon, why can't it be given by one of us?"

"Nickie, if you want to say anything, go ahead. But it better be pleasant. Everybody thinks a religious ceremony is appropriate. And certainly no cremation."

Sal nodded. "Mom was loved, after all, and, thank god, this

isn't Vietnam."

I looked at him, my fists clenched, and I swear, although we had not said an angry word in years, I was one syllable away from choking him. Sal's hair, and particularly his unshaved chin, looked terrible. Cora touched my shoulder and said the decision was not really ours, but our father's. "He wants it," she said. "Her family wants it." She looked at me. "Sal wants it, and I want it, too."

"Forget it," I finally said, unclenching my fists.

"Forget it? What—that she ever lived!"

Cora closed her eyes and tears rolled down her cheeks while Sal glared at me, taking her in his arms with soft moans and whispers. He stared at me over her shoulder, his eyes wet and red as Cora's, his jaw set and grim. "It *has* changed you," he said, quietly, looking at my uniform. "Well, it doesn't mean you know everything. It doesn't mean the change is for the better."

I said nothing. I stared at Cora, who stood huddled within his arms, and remarked to myself how slim she had become. Living in New York with her husband, Hank, she had begun to lose some of that natural, Jane Russell heft and develop a slim, more tailored figure. Solemnly, an older, more loyal sibling than either of them (I thought), I walked away, ignoring them both when they called my name.

I admit that during the next three days I began to have a change of heart. Walking around the house or the neighborhood, seeing the family at the funeral home, I searched for significance and felt along with Sal and Cora that something had to be made of my mother's passing. Despite all that I had seen recently, I could not stop a religious prayer from parting my lips when I first looked at her in the coffin each afternoon. She looked waxen, small. I saw myself in her dead body, thought about friends I had already lost, and didn't want to accept the frustration of her death as being her only end. Why had I survived so far? Why hadn't others? I kneeled before her casket, waiting for something to transform the sense of decay and silence into meaning. The flowers stank; the two families—hers, my father's—only served to make her death seem useless, impractical. It was not military—it did not have the startling energy and purpose of battle surrounding it—or the direction of political philosophy. Beside it, she and all of us who lived seemed hopelessly superficial.

"Well, Nickie, are you going to take good care of your father?" someone would ask. "You're all he's got."

I nodded, hearing that from almost all my aunts. Invariably it was followed by strong, matronly embraces and long looks at my face, my uniform, my ribbons. These were my parents' sisters (my father had nine of them; my mother, six), and although I gratefully accepted those embraces at first, the more they were given, the more I regarded them as pieces of theatre to keep me close to home. Family was all: I had sinned in leaving my mother to serve a larger power. My aunts flocked around my father's mother, who lived for years afterward and dominated her daughters and my father the way they dominated everyone else. By contrast, my mother's sisters, reflecting her position here, seemed retiring.

"What are you going to do now?" my Aunt Sarah asked. "Are you going back to the Army?"

"Marines," I said.

She was my father's sister, a big woman, intelligent, good-natured, and, as the film of my parents' twenty-fifth anniversary can only hint at, loud. "Marines. . . Whatever." She kissed me, embraced me, made me feel her tears against my neck. "Are you going back to that horrible place?"

"I have to," I lied, although I really didn't. "It's my job."

She stepped back and looked in my eyes. "What about your father and brother? Someone has to look after them. You're the oldest."

I shrugged. "I haven't thought about it yet," I said. "Sal's alright. And with my father, there's always Cora to help."

"Still, you're the oldest. You have to do these things."

Aunt Sarah embraced me again—but very carefully, insistently, I pulled away. Boots, helmet, and combat uniform were gone, but as they used to insist in Quantico, you can take the Marine out of combat, but never the combat out of a good Marine. I kissed her, coolly, properly, my hands on her shoulders, keeping her huge body at arms' length.

"If you ever need anything, Nickie, just remember your Aunt Sarah. I'm your godmother after all."

Without an instant's hesitation, I dropped my hands, placed my right foot behind my left, did an about face, and walked onto the porch of the funeral home to smoke—yes, Mayra—to smoke a joint.

"What home was I fighting for?"

VIII

That day and the one following were a series of scenes like that, and I have often tried to tell Mayra about them. As the family filed past the coffin, looked at my mother, kneeling to say brief prayers, I felt increasingly embarrassed and bitter. If this was the end, what had I flown ten-thousand miles to fight for? It's easy to say my attitude was a result of my mother's passing, or the war: too much blood and violence, too much death. But it was more than that. The wake, its emotions, my angry, jealous thinking about my comfortable brother and sister, both of whom looked at me as if I didn't belong, worked to push me deeper into my own private gloom.

My father, on the other hand, felt better as the days went by. Except for the quiet, mournful crying that he fell into upon entering the funeral home each day, he stayed close to his family and talked easily to his mother and others. He even joked occasionally with some of the visitors, and by the night before the interment he looked pretty much himself. We came home late and talked in the kitchen with Sal before going to bed. He poured a shot of rye whisky for each of the three of us and heated a cup of milk on the stove for himself. We turned on the radio for some music. I remember the Beatles coming on, not the song but their singing, and then a long, slow ballad of protest by a woman whose voice called to mind brooks, tall grass, and naked feet running through both while promising commitment and lifelong love as soon as the fighting in that stranger's "far-off, broken" land began to stop.

The three of us sat at the table, overwhelmed by the dark passion of her voice, the words it gave feeling to, and I, thinking of the land surrounding our own wife and mother's grave, knew that for us, or one of us at least, the fighting would likely never stop.

It was a difficult four or five minutes. The white light from the overhead fixture threw everything into relief, and suddenly the prospect of new life for a bereft father and two sons seemed hopelessly impoverished. My father sipped at the milk and the rye, loosened his tie, and rolled up his sleeves. I looked at Sal and smiled as he swallowed his whisky, and he, shifting his gaze to the ceiling, merely shook his head and slumped, as if a weight had been loaded on, and then taken off, his shoulders.

"There's a lot of room in the house," my father said hopefully. "The three of us could be very comfortable. You boys are welcome as long as you like."

He squeezed Sal's shoulder and patted my arm, saying, "I mean it," and kissed my cheek. Seeing tears in both his and my brother's eyes, I flinched, not because of love, but because I felt confined.

After a few seconds I kissed him back and said, "Thanks, Pop. I'll probably finish my tour. I'm on short time now, and it's nice to know I can come back here."

Sal said nothing, but out of the corner of my eye I could see him watching me. My father nodded. We finished our drinks and bid each other good-night. Sal went off to be with his girlfriend, telling me not to wait up for him, and so I sat up alone, as I often would in the next six months, smoking, rocking in a cane chair at least as old as I was, catching up to the latest music and listening to the noises of the house as I thought about Vietnam. My company came to mind, one or two real buddies who had been in country with me since the beginning. We had passed through some good times, and I thought of a few of them, some gross situations and jokes that were awful but had a veneer of hilarity about them because they took place over there.

I was happier in the Marines than I had ever been at home, and I knew it. Despite all my bitching, I could not deny the edge, the chill, even the fear in anticipation of putting everything, mind, soul, body, on the line for country and self. But what home was I fighting for if I did not wish to live there? What life, if it ended up in the ground, like my mother's? I had awful, awful thoughts, ones I could never tell anyone, least of all father and brother (or, later, wife and daughter). Suffice to say that the saner side of me wondered what I had been born to do if pointing a gun, pulling a trigger, and smashing a skull were the main pleasures and accomplishments of my life.

IX

I read quite a bit on the long flight home: letters, my mother's letters. We had not been close, mainly because I did not want to be, was not my mother's type of boy. Still, I received quite a few letters from her once I went away. During my fifteen months in country, she seemed to open up to me, tell me in letters things she had never revealed before: the difficulties she had loving my father, the temptations of men in her life, and, most revealing, an important affair, one with my favorite teacher, during which she actually stayed away from the house for several weeks, leaving my father and Cora to cope with Sal and me.

Perhaps it was the miles between us; perhaps she knew somehow her death was near. Or perhaps, as my wife Valerie once said to me, she simply never had anybody to write to before, making confession hard to resist. Whatever, she poured herself into those letters, telling me things I preferred not knowing, describing scenes from her youth and age I preferred not imagining, and yet as the MATS plane crossed the International Dateline that day after Tet, I felt grateful to her for the news. She had seen New York and Miami; she had crossed the ocean to Rome, stood praying in Vatican Square, handkerchief on her head, purse clutched in her hand, and stared at that balcony window for an hour to see the "chubby little Pope," as she called him, finally come to the railing and extend his hand.

All this while I thought she was in the hospital with, as the family called it, "woman troubles." My father, quiet, stoic, or perhaps simply ashamed, went through those days listlessly but methodically, rousing us from bed, feeding us, and driving us to school before going off to his own job. At night he and Cora

41

cooked, and on weekends, both Saturday and Sunday, he took us to Aunt Sarah's for dinner. Sal, Cora, and I played with our cousins and when the adults' voices suddenly dropped as we entered their company, we assumed they were discussing my mother. But we thought, once again, her "woman troubles" occupied the conversation.

"I have lived so many lives," she wrote about a month before she died, "but nothing like the one I had during that week and a half in Rome with Aaron."

Aaron, or Mr. Zuder, as I knew him, was my fifth grade shop and crafts teacher, a man who loved wood, especially cherry and oak, and knew how to coax the most exquisite shapes and surfaces out of it, either by hand carving or lathe. A handsome, fleshy bachelor with a reputation for strictness among the students, he took my mother to Rome to visit the major sights but ended up preferring the small towns outside the city because their churches held more carved wood than marble. He had proposed to my mother in the sacristy of one of them, and even though she refused (he must have known she would: she couldn't leave her family for good, she told me), in the square afterward he bought her a foot-high statue of the Madonna and Child that had been carved from Italian chestnut. She had carried it in her bag when she returned to my father, but "out of respect" for him and her children, as she said to me, she left it in the attic, only to see it once or twice, usually around Christmas, in the following years.

There had been others, but Mr. Zuder was the one who stuck, she told me, always ready to welcome her into another life, "of travel, or passion," that she could never choose over her family. My father did nothing, suffering the sudden departures because, apparently, he had his own vices, though she never complained of them or told me what they were.

The one reminder of that adventure, she told me, was the print of the cherry trees that hung above our living room couch. After they returned, she had bought it for Mr. Zuder at a local art shop. But he had refused it, saying he couldn't take the print if she did not want to live with him. So she hung it in our house, our living room centerpiece, its pink, blossomy scene a comment on a part of life that she always wanted but couldn't keep.

X

The morning of the funeral was sunny and hot. I felt relieved it was the last day I would have to wear my Class A's. When we entered the funeral home, my father and I kneeled before the coffin, and he, crossing himself after a moment, reached into it to pat my mother's hand. He had brought her diamond-studded wedding ring ("the dressy one," she called it) and asked the undertaker to put it on in place of the plain gold one she was wearing.

Unassuming and efficient as when we first met, my old school chum Digger Di nodded solemnly, but at the coffin he had difficulty. The old ring came off easily, but the diamond one, despite all his pushing and pulling, would not go on. My mother had always had trouble with that ring herself, which is why she only wore it on special occasions. Frequently, after a party or relatively formal dinner, she had to soak her hands in soap and water to free it. Sometimes it took several hours. So, we watched, horrified, as Digger, turning his back to us for cover, pushed and pulled at her ring finger. After a few minutes, he dropped his hands and asked the family to leave the room.

"Why?" I demanded, though everyone else seemed more than willing to cooperate. "Are you going to break her finger—or cut it off?"

"No! No, Nick, don't be silly. I would just feel more comfortable if the family weren't watching. For his sake." Digger nodded toward my father.

"It's okay, Nickie. Let him do it."

Shaking my head, and with visions of Vietnam atrocities, I left the room and waited with my father in the vestibule. Other members of the family arrived: Cora and her husband, Hank, a few aunts and uncles, all of whom shook our hands and said something about me or my uniform. We waited more than fifteen minutes with the door to the room closed. When Digger opened it finally, my father, Sal, and I took the three seats nearest the coffin. I saw the diamond ring on my mother's finger (the gold one had been slipped into my father's jacket pocket as we entered), but later I discovered that Digger had cut the ring open to make a proper fit. I was outraged, fuming, but as usual, my father was more reasonable: "It doesn't matter now," he told me. "As long as she has it with her."

I intended to complain to Digger anyway, but as I went to find him my grandmother arrived on the arm of Uncle Ralph, and after helping him support her as she stood and prayed before the coffin, I completely forgot about the ring.

My grandmother made that happen. Prayer finished, she took the seat next to my father but held on to my hand. She studied me, her large, dark eyes virtually peering through me, trying to understand, I thought: the uniform, the ribbons, the absence of mourning black.

"*Come stai?*" she asked, not blinking behind her glasses. "You feel okay today?"

"*Sta bene, Nona.*" I pulled my hand away. But she leaned toward me, and, thinking she wanted another kiss, I pecked her cheek.

"No, no," she said, pulling back. "One is enough. I want to look at you." She took hold of my sleeve. "You're a big boy now, a soldier. You have to take care of your father."

I nodded, my chest unconsciously expanding despite a wish to turn and run. After a long moment, she asked what I was planning to do.

"Do? When?"

"With your father, now that your mother has died."

I shook my head. "I haven't thought about it yet, Nona."

She looked doubtful and squeezed my wrist, hard. Struggling for words in English, she said, "You and your father, you have each other now. You take care of him, but who is going to take care of you?"

"I'm a man now, Nona. Don't worry. Besides, Sal and Cora will help." I kissed her cheek a second time and, embarrassed, started to move away. But she held my wrist, not letting me leave.

"Nickie, Nickie. What are we going to do with you?" She smiled, her eyes very deep and serious. Settling back in her chair, she looked at the coffin for a few seconds. "You don't know what it means to be without a mother, Nickie. You think hard what you want to do."

"I will, Nona. Thanks."

I kissed her, or tried to, a third time. But she turned her cheek away, and my lips touched nothing but her hair. Blushing and laughing at myself, I stood up to greet some people just walking through the door.

The room was nearly filled now. In a few minutes Digger Di came in with Father Rossi and introduced him to me and the rest of the family. Correct but distant, I shook the priest's hand and tried to measure him for sincerity. There was very little to observe, I thought. He wore a dark suit and hat, which he took off and handed to Digger without looking. His thin, prominent nose gave him a suspicious, bird-like appearance while his voice, deep and confident, bespoke an acquaintance with enthralled, captive audiences. At the same time, both his bald head and wire-rimmed glasses threw off flashes of light, as if he were used to the dramatic pose at center stage. He leaned toward my father, talked with him and my grandmother a few minutes, to my mind avoiding the coffin. A hush had settled over the room since he entered, a respectful reaction to his collar that made me very, very uncomfortable. I still harbored illusions of making a funeral oration, I confess, but nobody had asked, and I lacked nerve or confidence enough to suggest it myself. Instead in a few minutes I watched enviously while Digger presented to the audience this stranger who, through confession, probably knew more about my mother's life than I did and, in addition, stood to receive from the family the attention I secretly coveted.

He drew a scarlet maniple from his jacket pocket and draped it over his collar. With a bowed head, he took a Bible out, opened it to a pre-selected passage and, the maniple flashing in the lights along with his glasses, raised his hand with a flourish. The hush in the room immediately deepened to absolute silence.

"Friends," he said. "And I call you friends, though I haven't met many of you before; it is sad to come together today, even though it is spring. This good woman has departed, leaving in grief husband, children and grandchildren, and all the rest who are friends and relatives. These are hard moments, particularly for you, Nicholas, and yes, you, my good lady, the mother of this now forsaken son. But remember that the good Lord always provides, and in this long moment of life, He is always prepared to help us in our solitude.

"Don't despair, I say. Don't lose hope, Nicholas. Despair is one of the deadliest of sins, and I say to you today that should you lose hope you will have given up your trust in Divinity. The deceased . . . Sophie, led a rich, full life. And I assure you that although she is taken from us now, perhaps a little before her allotted time, she will live in the memory of her beloved husband, children, and the rest of us who gather here today. Life is indeed rich when we remember those who have gone before us. We may be grateful to God that He has created this woman, nourished her through years of youth and maturity, and now escorts her into the light of His angels' eyes. May we all live up to her performance, and may we all see her again when we too have passed beyond this valley to the other, kindlier one. Now, my friends, join me while I pray."

He turned, kneeling before the coffin, and I swear I saw him glance at his watch before re-opening his Bible. This was when I lost perspective. On my knees with the rest, I felt myself tremble with laughter, almost ready to call out something perverse. My mother looked pathetic in the coffin, surrounded

by flowers though she was and paid respect by such a large
assembly of people. It struck me as wrong that in a few minutes
Digger would close the coffin lid, and we would never see her
again, never make up for the wrongs that we, she, and the
courses of our lives, had inflicted on each other. She had not
been happy; her life had been more frustrating than meaningful,
and I sincerely wondered how much I had contributed to her
misery. Having lived a bare fifty-five years, she had just a few
moments of laughter in a life that I saw as ending without
regrets. There were moments when I thought of her in the
ground, her flesh decaying slowly and painfully, and identifying
her with that woman in Vietnam, I felt I might lose control.
When I tried to block such thoughts from my mind, I looked at
Father Rossi's darting head, heard what I imagined was a lack of
commitment behind his words, and almost cried out until I
looked at my mother and felt a real sense of relief. Her
troubles were over.

Father Rossi stood after he finished, and people began to
file past him to the coffin. My father left his seat first, but
Digger officiously motioned him back to his chair and waved to
those in the back of the room to come ahead. I heard a whine,
quiet but gradually growing louder; when I looked around I saw
my grandmother passing my father a handkerchief. He took it,
weakly dabbing his eyes and nose, casting a miserable glance at
my mother in the coffin. With her hand on his shoulder, my
grandmother whispered in his ear. He nodded. "I'm sorry,
Sophie," he said aloud. "I should have gone first. Don't leave
me."

Sal and I took my grandmother by either arm and stood by
her side as she said her final, inaudible good-bye. We escorted
her to the vestibule then returned and stood together beside the
coffin. "Good-bye," Sal muttered. Then, almost sportingly,
"Good journey." I said nothing, mainly because my throat was
full and I couldn't sort out my words. Sal looked at me. I
looked at him and, after a moment, nodded. Without kissing

her, we turned together toward my father and extended our hands.

He was silent, roughly pushing us aside as he walked to the coffin on his own. His eyes were clear, his head slightly cocked, and, as if he wanted to memorize something, he studied her with a quiet, I would have to say loving, adoration. He kneeled and stared as if he couldn't believe who she was. Sal and I stood behind but like Digger, who watched cautiously from the door, we were prepared to stop him from any rashness. I rested my hand on his shoulder, and after a few quiet seconds, he stood up. In tears, he leaned over to kiss her mouth. His voice became high, pleading. It was a sound I could not listen to.

"Oh, we'll miss you, Sophie. We'll be lost without you."

As he clung to her dress and pawed her diamond-studded ring, I gently, with Digger's nodding approval, pulled him away. He withdrew reluctantly, walking into the hall, but I turned back just before Digger closed the coffin.

"Wait a minute. I haven't done this yet." I bent over and kissed her on the cheek. Without warning, a sob burst from my throat and tears flooded my eyes. I squinted them back, clamped my mouth, and, after an angry glance at Digger, left the room.

The air was brisk outside. The sun shined pleasantly through the newly budding trees. Although I lacked a philosophic or religious focus on my mother's death, the fact that it was spring, that it was an incredibly warm and beautiful morning, provided a natural structure where—for the time at least—emotions took the place of words. The earth was soft, muddy, establishing a new growing year. From this perspective, the burial became a means of participating in life or, at least, touching a source of it. But of course, as a soldier I knew something about the false images nature could project.

"You know which car we sit in?" Sal said. He stood beside me on the sidewalk, nervously shifting his feet while staring past me to the street. Limousines lined the curb, with a flower car in the lead. The hearse, which we all kept waiting for, stayed

in the driveway until Digger's pallbearers brought my mother to
it.

"We take the front cars, don't we?" said my brother-in-law
Hank, emerging from some people near the steps. "Those are
for the immediate family, I think."

He grimaced and shuffled a little, his hands behind his
back. We watched as more family cars pulled to the curb behind
the limousines, and then at last the hearse left the driveway,
stopping in front of the flower car while the pallbearers
carried the coffin to it. The moment was ominous. My mother
always grew roses in our backyard, and she had sent several
snapshots to me in Nam, of her among them on sunny
afternoons. As a soldier, I had felt the photographs powerfully,
especially after hearing that she was ill. As a mourning son I
could not even think of them. In the photographs she had worn
her white hair cut short and set in a tight permanent wave. Her
smile had struck me as relaxed and open, even though she and
everyone else knew she was not well or happy. Still, with the
roses, the smile, the hair shining in the sun, I had, in war,
allowed myself to feel some hope.

Shortly Hank, Sal, and I went to the limousines, entering
the first one with my father, Cora, and my grandmother. A gray
limousine, with Digger, the priest, and the pallbearers in it,
drove ahead of the hearse, leading us at a slow pace through the
center of town, then out of it again until we reached the
cemetery just beyond town limits. I watched my father as we
rode, noting how calm he had become. He talked quietly in
Italian with my grandmother, pointing to familiar landmarks
and discussing them with her.

The gray limousine slowed at the entrance to the cemetery
and waited while the rest of the procession caught up. Then
gradually it led us along the winding roads until we came to a
slope just before some railroad tracks. It was the last, most
open part of the cemetery, with a view of grass, trees, and, in
the distance, the main road that passed by. It seemed an

appropriate spot for some reason. I have liked to think of my mother there because of the space and the sense of life and movement. Even the railroad track contributes something: In my imagination the whistle blowing at night reflects the energies and longings of my parents' lives.

My father started from the car immediately, but Digger trotted over and told us all to wait until the full line of cars had come to a stop. We watched the pallbearers, with Father Rossi following, bring the casket to the grave. Men with shovels stood near a pile of dirt, leaving when the pallbearers placed the casket on the ground. Then Digger nodded, and one of the drivers arrived to open car doors and tell us to get out. My father scrambled from his seat immediately, breaking into a trot across the grass. Sal and I helped my grandmother and followed.

Strangely, I kept waiting for something to happen, a special event—wonderful or awful—to mark the occasion. And, I confess, despite my uniform I was relieved to be unarmed, for inside, something was losing shape. When the priest raised the crucifix, I half expected the coffin lid to fly open and see my mother step out to announce her love for Mr. Zuder. Then, as Father Rossi started to pray, a V of geese flew over, honking, and I found myself nodding and laughing at them, as if I understood. I remembered groves of deep green foliage concealing dismembered bodies and thriving, blood-spattered plants with fingers, toes, or genitals beneath them; or cows, grazing and chewing contentedly as other animals, or humans, screamed and died. This was a mistake. A lie. We must not shovel an ounce of dirt on that coffin.

I looked at my father, his head bowed, sobbing into my grandmother's handkerchief, and out of reflex felt angry and muddled at the same time. I knew it was perfectly human not to be able to deal competently with death. With all my experience, I knew there was no real answer to it all, yet I couldn't understand why I was the only one who seemed to feel uncertain. I might have screamed if someone crossed me. And if someone gave me a reason, even a small one, funeral or not I would have gone at him or her with my bare hands.

Still, the others seemed accepting, the pattern of their eye movements betraying only slight ambivalence: Father Rossi to the casket, then back to Father Rossi again, interspersing that with occasional random glances at the sky.

It was an empty few minutes, worse than all the hours at the funeral parlor. I tried to master the time by thinking of pleasant, natural things, roses, pendulums, cycles, gyres, anything to counteract the one-way movement I had seen in my mother's life. But war memories interrupted and I could only understand every amazing thing that had happened in the last few years with an idea that seemed too banal and obvious: the ultimate victory of nature over everything, the triumph of grass, undergrowth, and trees.

"We shall *rise*!" Father Rossi shouted. "The Lord promises in His Book. We shall *rise*!—And his Son will take each of us by the hand. So have hope Nicholas and his children; hope that you will see this wife and mother again and join with her in God's eternal love."

In the context of such reflections, Father Rossi consigned my mother's body to the grave and with a flourish of the crucifix stepped back as Digger's aids lowered the casket into the ground. Digger passed out stems of carnations and motioned to my aunts to place them on the coffin as they filed past. I didn't want to see or hear the stones and dirt hit the wooden lid, and was relieved, after dropping my flower on the slowly gathering pile, when Digger motioned everyone toward the limousines. In the confusion that followed, some searched for their cars, some stopped to shake hands, others left to meet at our house for a post-funeral luncheon. As I walked toward our limousine, Digger called my name, "Nickie," and automatically I pointed to my father as the senior person.

"No, I want to speak to you, Nick." He shook his head.

When I motioned to my father again, Digger pointed at me. "This is for you. I have to show you something important."

"Digger," I said, clenching my fists, "I'm not ready—"

"Nick, please."

He raised his finger to his lips and took my arm to lead me back to the site of the grave. The men had raised a lean-to to cover the work of filling it in. Digger pulled aside a flap of the lean-to and stepped behind it, motioning me in after him. I heard the thud of gravel and stones on wood and, scared as well as impatient, looked away.

"Come here, Nick, I want to show you this."

"Digger, please. . ."

"Look—the vault," he said. I stepped inside the lean-to and nodded. The men stood there, shoveling, smoking, now and then bending and tossing aside the flowers. They were quiet and respectful enough, but I was afraid of bizarre jokes being told and didn't want to listen to their humor. I started to leave again, but Digger held me back.

"Wait. Look, Nick. Here. It's concrete."

He lifted a portion of the ground cloth and pointed beneath it to something in the shadows. "Come here. I want you to see, so there won't be any disagreement later on. I want your family to like our work." He took my hand, rubbing it against a concrete slab that protruded slightly from the ground. It was the vault. In the corner, beneath the edge of the ground cover, I also saw the brown mahogany stain of my mother's coffin. For the moment, it seemed alive.

"The vault's cement; complete, four sides and the bottom," Digger said.

I felt impatient and confused, scared to the point of immobility. When Digger tapped my arm and pointed to the vault again, I turned on him suddenly, my fists before me, and with my chest and legs pushed him against the lean-to pole. Holding my breath, I said, "Terrific, Digger. But what's it for?"

His glasses flashed in the light, and he spoke, gently, I must admit. "I'm sorry, Nickie, but someone should know these things. It's a wooden box, but no rain will get in. No water from underground. The, ah. . .; your, ah. . .; it will stay dry."

"The casket?" I said.

"The uh . . ."

It dawned on me. With a note of stupid triumph I shouted, "Oh, no! No! Even Digger Di, the Friendly Undertaker, has his emotions!"

He shrugged, now looking impatient and confused himself. "It's in the contract, Nick. Some people question it when we send the bill. By then, of course, it's too late. Like Mr. Zuder used to tell us, you have to finish things right, completely, according to contract."

"Mr. Zuder said that?" I looked at him.

"You remember Mr. Zuder, the shop teacher: a perfectionist, a real stickler for details."

I said nothing. We started back to the cars together, smiling.

"I owe him a lot," Digger said.

At the road I shook his hand and Father Rossi's—telling the priest he'd delivered a well-constructed sermon. And although I wasn't ready to crack completely, I was close. I needed to hide, couldn't wait, in fact, to enter our limousine. Sal and Cora sat there. Hank, my father, and grandmother had switched to a family car to go directly to our house. As I got in, a jet flew overhead, breaking the sound barrier. Barely suppressing a shout—and giggle—after the sonic boom, I sat next to Cora and, wordless, held her arm.

She, Sal, and I looked at each other in silence as the driver started the engine and drove away.